CHARE

A NOVELLA

PENN ANDERSON

Printed in the United States of America

First Printing, 2026

Library of Congress Control Number: 2026903748

ISBN 979-8-9887493-2-5 (Large-print paperback)
ISBN 979-8-9887493-3-2 (eBook)

www.PennAnderson.com

for Joanie

1. Bobby
2. The Getaway Car
3. The Piper Family
4. Yarn and Justice
5. Ron

BOBBY

Chare was never meant to be alone. She was one of a hundred identical siblings. A "pack animal" through and through. She had never spent a night alone, never gone anywhere without at least ten members of her family, and never been singled out for anything, let alone her looks. At fourteen years old, it was the first time she felt the coach's hands on her. The scary part was over in a flash. Fifty feet in 2.1 seconds. It was done. She was intact. Bruised, rattled, exhilarated, and blessedly intact. But what nobody knew was that Chare's restoration would take a lifetime, and her spectacular journey was just beginning.

In 1971, the Indiana University Athletics Department purchased a set of one hundred red molded plastic chairs.
In February of 1985, basketball coach Bobby Knight threw one of those chairs across the court as an expression of outrage over a referee's call. This is her story.

(The chair, I mean.)

Chare lay on her side in the corner of the court, close to a row of crouched photographers. She watched as the referees convened in the chaos. The cheers of "Bob-by! Bob-by!" were deafening, shouted in solidarity with the angry man who had done this. Chare felt a painful twist in her back left leg, and the screw at its origin was now aimed directly into her red plastic bottom instead of the metal threaded hole.

"Get this out of the way," a man said,

turning back to the game, arms crossed. A tall woman carried Chare by the neck and set her right-side-up in the hallway just outside the court. Chare regained her equilibrium and tried to listen to the rest of the game. Before long, she was grabbed again, this time by a man. He jogged with her down the hallway, around a corner, and down three steps. She had never seen this part of the arena. The man tried to open two doors but they were both locked. He tried a third, and as it swung open, he squeezed Chare's neck harder. "Perfect," he said. He tossed her into this room, the boiler room, and ran back to the game.

Chare was alone.

In the very first instant of the dramatic skid across the court, Chare and her sister had briefly tangled their front feet, and in doing so, pulled two or three other siblings out of position, too. Now, scared and upside-down in the dusty corner of the loud boiler room, Chare focused on the particular warmth of that small round foot. The foot her sister had tried to grab. That fading warmth was all she had left of her family, and all she would ever have.

The crowd was so incensed and maniacal, Ron had to lean in close to his daughter's ear for her to hear him. "Gwennie, I know you know this. But that's not the way to solve problems."

Gwen looked up at him and rolled her eyes. "I know, Dad." She scooted another inch away from him on the bleacher and took a drink of her soda.

Ron looked back at the court and watched as the Purdue kid attempted six free throws, the penalty for the technical fouls called on Coach, who had been ejected from the game.

Thankfully, he only made three of the shots.

"No, I mean it, Gwen. It's important. Before you know it, you're gonna be dating. Spending time with...*people*."

"People?"

"Well, I was gonna say men, but I don't know if it'll be men or women so I don't want to make assumptions." Ron saw the couple in front of him turn around slightly, and then give each other a look.

"Dad, don't be weird."

"Look, you just want to make sure and pay attention to how people handle tough situations. Watch out for that temper. It can start with little things at first. Reactions in traffic. The way they speak to a waiter."

"For the record, I'm only twelve."

"I know."

"Ha. *Do* you know? Cuz you kinda missed the whole birthday thing."

Ron looked at Gwen and moved uncomfortably in his seat. The comment was a dagger, but he knew he deserved it. He sat up straighter. "Yeah. Yeah, I know. I'm really sorry about that."

"Seems like you're sorry a lot lately."

Gwen was holding her lucky guitar pick between her thumb and forefinger, rubbing it like a worry stone. The judge had only given Ron visitation with his daughter one weekend a month, and he always tried to plan something special for their time together, even though he could barely afford it. About a year before, he had taken her to a John Cougar Mellencamp concert. Gwen had found a guitar pick by her feet and was convinced it was Mellencamp's. Since that night, she brought it with her everywhere, and she had also started playing acoustic guitar. In only a few months, she had already made it through advanced songbooks and she was recommended to study with a guitar professor at the University. With a jolt, Ron remembered his half of the bill for her guitar lessons was still sitting on his kitchen table.

"Look, I'll make it up to you." Ron paused, unsure what he could offer. And unsure of what he could say that wouldn't push her further away. "Hey, this game is pretty fun, right? You'll have a story at school next week, that's for sure."

Gwen didn't answer. Ron noticed in the corner of the court, the chair was being removed and carried up a courtside tunnel. "There goes a new piece of Hoosier history. Coach should sign it."

"I'm kinda surprised you're still a fan," she said.

"Huh? What do you mean? I'm their *biggest* fan."

"Didn't they fire you, though?"

"Well..." Ron looked down at his lap and lowered his voice. He had been working on the custodial staff here at Assembly Hall for three years, but had lost his job in the fall, just before this basketball season had started. "That was all a misunderstanding. I'm pretty sure I can get my job back. We're just taking a break."

"But didn't you show up...." Gwen snaked her arms out of her jean jacket, rolled it up and set it under her seat, as if she were stalling. "I mean...didn't you show up to work...drunk?" The couple sitting in front of them turned around again.

“The game’s that way,” Ron said to them, irritated, pointing at the court.

“Gwen,” Ron said quietly. He reached over to lift a loose pink thread off the knee of her jeans, but she flinched away from him. He took a long, deep breath. “Your mother tell you that?”

“Well, is it true?”

Ron didn’t answer, and they barely spoke the rest of the game. Whenever Ron wanted to say something, it felt like his tongue was made of clay. His words and promises meant nothing to her anymore—rightly so. Nothing he could say would make Gwen understand. Nothing could make Gwen adore him like she did when she was a little girl. He had thrown away so much. So much time… lost. The divorce. The drinking. The debts. And every time he thought he had almost climbed his way back out, some unlucky break would push him off his foothold.

"I'm sober now, Gwennie. I promise you."

What Gwen didn't know, and what she never would have believed at that moment, was that Ron had been sober since the day he was fired, and he would never take another drink again. He would hold a steady government job, pull himself out of debt, and build a good long life. Ron himself might not have believed it, either. But he knew he had let Gwen down too many times, and that night he vowed to do better. Gwen mattered more to him than anyone or anything in the world. It was that night, at the iconic "Chair Game," when he made it his mission to make up for lost time with her. What he could picture was so beautiful. He would go to her school events and her guitar recitals. He would take her photo on a grassy lawn on prom night. He would build a lofted bed frame for her college dorm room. He would shake her fiancé's hand, firmly. He would hold a newborn grandchild, middle name Ronald. He could see it all so clearly. But what Ron didn't know, and what he never would have believed at that moment, was that he and Gwen had only one day left together. After that, Ron wouldn't see his daughter again for thirty-five years.

"Dad, turn around!" Gwen shrieked as she sat up straight and grabbed the car's dashboard with both hands.

"What the hell? You're gonna give me a heart attack, girl."

"My jacket! I forgot my jacket. I know right where it is. I put it under the bleachers. Turn around! We have to go back!"

"Aww, Gwen, really? It's so late. Look at this snarl I'm in. How am I supposed to turn around? And what's this?" He reached over and tugged on the fabric of her winter coat.

"No, my *jean* jacket. Remember? You

made me wear this coat on top of it." Gwen started to cry. "I'm really sorry I forgot it, but please can you just go back?" She was almost hyperventilating.

"OK, don't cry, honey. I'll do what I can. But I don't know if we'll even be able to get back inside the arena." He hoped she hadn't heard the frustration in his voice. "This just might take a while."

"Thanks, Dad." Gwen got out a Hershey bar she had put in the glove box and broke off a section for each of them. The lanes of cars were at a total standstill.

Ron looked in his mirrors and managed to get over to the exit lane, only receiving a couple of honks. He got on the freeway again, heading back to Assembly Hall. Just the two miles took almost forty minutes, and Ron was trying to think how to approach the building with the best chance of finding an open door. Fortunately, he saw that a few fans were still exiting through the main doors and he decided to park in a close spot reserved for the Chancellor.

"We really have to hustle, Gwen, OK?"

"Got it, Dad. Thanks." They jogged up to

the doors, through the lobby, and down the hallway to the stairs. Taking them two at a time, they entered their seating section completely out of breath.

“Shoot! Gwen, that’s our row.” Ron was crouching down. “I can see from here it’s not there. Someone must have already put it in lost and found. Come with me!” They ran back down the stairs. The arena was almost deserted. Maybe a dozen people were left in the entire place. “This way. Brenda might still be here.” They jogged down a long hallway to the office.

"Ronald? Is that you?" a voice called from behind them, and they stopped running.

"Brenda! Boy, are we glad to see you. We need to check lost and found."

"Ronald, you shouldn't be here," she said.

"No, no, it's OK. We were at the game. This is my daughter." Ron dug around for his ticket stub but couldn't find it. "Look, you gotta believe me. We just came back to find her jacket."

Brenda looked at Gwen's winter coat and back at Ron.

"Brenda, please. Could you just help me out here? Please."

She sighed, and pulled a large set of keys attached to a retractable cord away from her waistband. She walked in front of them and escorted them down another hallway to the office.

"You have exactly thirty seconds, Ronald," she said, while standing in the doorway like a lookout.

"There it is!" Gwen exclaimed. She ran to the box and held the jacket up to her face like a baby blanket. "Oh, Dad! Thank you!"

"Thank God," muttered Ron. "Thanks, Brenda. I owe you one." Brenda rolled her eyes and locked the door behind them. She walked in the other direction towards the staff parking lot. Ron and Gwen almost skipped back towards the main doors, feeling like giddy co-conspirators, but also because the empty hall was a little eerie and they were eager to get home.

"Wait, let me put this on." Gwen stopped short. She took off her winter coat and held it between her knees as she put on her jean jacket. She put her hands in her jacket pockets and swung them around like she had just donned a fur coat. But then she froze in place, with a look of horror. The winter coat dropped to the floor.

"What is it?"

Gwen looked up at her Dad. "The guitar pick. It's not here."

"Maybe it's in the other coat." He picked

it up off the floor and looked through the pockets.

"No, I always carry it in this little pocket of the jean jacket. It's not here." Gwen looked stricken. "Can we go back to the office? Is Brenda still here? Or can we go look up in the stands? Please, Dad!"

"Honey, I can get you another pick just like that one." Most of the lights in the arena were off now. Ron looked down the length of the lonely hallway. His eye caught a flash of red.

"Hey! What are you doing?" Ron shouted

and took off running down the hallway, Gwen's winter coat still in his hand.

"Dad!" Gwen wailed after him. She started running to catch up.

"That doesn't belong to you!" Ron called after the man carrying the red plastic chair. Ron had just seen the man carry it out of the boiler room and start running with it to the back doors—the catering entrance. Ron was gaining on him.

"Stop!" Ron called again. The man pushed open the double doors and clattered the chair through them. Ron burst through behind him and dove, grabbing a hold of one leg of the chair. The man turned and kicked Ron hard, pounding his foot into the side of Ron's left knee. Ron yelled out in pain, but didn't let go. The two men each held an opposing silver leg of the chair, as if they were about to break a wishbone. Ron held on tight as he tried to get to his feet.

"Where do you think you're going with this, buddy?" Ron wiped his arm across his face and realized his nose was bleeding. He touched his nostril and wiped the blood on his jeans.

"None of your business, asshole." The man

ripped the chair from Ron's hand and tried to run again. Ron managed to lunge for the neck of the man's jacket, pulling him backwards in a chokehold. The man dropped the chair and put both of his hands in the air.

"Jesus, fine. Take it. It's just a chair, you psychopath."

Ron kept a tight hold on the man's jacket and slowly reached down with his free hand to grab the chair.

"I don't want to see you around here again. Do you understand?" Ron released his hold on the collar and the man ran away. Ron stood and watched, breathing hard, with the chair hanging like a scalp from his blood-streaked hand, until he saw the man get into a white Jeep and drive away.

Ron winced and reached down to hold his knee. When he finally stood up and turned around, he saw the smallest frame of a girl, standing in front of a door, looking at him, eyes wide. She was illuminated perfectly from above by a bright yellow security light. She wore the jean jacket she had worn to her first concert. He watched her turn around slowly, and push on a locked door.

It was 10:00 a.m. when Gwen finally walked into the kitchen, still in her pajamas, not making eye contact with her dad. She opened the refrigerator to get out the orange juice. The waffles Ron had made earlier were now cold and unappealing, piled on a plate in the center of the round kitchen table, next to an open can of diced pineapple.

"Morning, sweetie."

Silence.

"Hey, so I was thinking, what we can do is go back to the arena and look for your guitar pick after breakfast. Things will be reconfigured for practice today but we should be able to get in. Then I can drop you off at your mom's."

"Where's your precious chair?" Gwen asked, scanning the kitchen and living room.

"Look, I know that whole thing must have looked ridiculous."

Gwen stared at him coldly. She gave him nothing.

"It's still in the back seat of my car. I'm gonna return it today and explain that the doors were locked and we couldn't get back in last night."

"I bet that conversation will go smoothly." Gwen grabbed a waffle and ate it while looking out the window.

"That guy was taking something that didn't belong to him, Gwen. He probably would have turned around and sold it. The infamous chair. Someone would pay a lot for that chair. Like five grand, I'm guessing. You know it's all over the news today?"

"Wow, how does it feel to be a hero?" she said, without affect.

"I wasn't..."

Gwen cut him off. "What was all that stuff about staying away from guys who can't keep their cool?"

"That's true, Gwen. Look, I'm sorry you had to see that. It's complicated, OK?"

"Oh, please explain."

"I was thinking about this while I was trying to fall asleep last night. I guess...I guess maybe I was trying to prove I was still on their team. That I was still a Hoosier. A loyalty thing, you know? And maybe they'd give me my job back. I don't know. I guess that sounds stupid. It felt like I was doing it for *you.*"

"You're right, that does sound stupid. I'm gonna get dressed. We don't have time to go to the arena. I told you, I have my friend's birthday party at noon. Just drop me at Mom's and she'll take me over there."

Gwen carried her dishes to the sink and disappeared to her bedroom. Ron heard the water running and then the sounds of Gwen getting her bag together. He straightened up the kitchen and started to feel the first icy tingles of her pending absence.

"It wasn't lucky, anyway," she said as she emerged from her room wearing her backpack.

"What?"

"The guitar pick. It wasn't lucky. It probably wasn't even Mellencamp's. I'm over it. Let's just go." She had already opened the back kitchen door that led to the alley behind Ron's apartment. He followed behind her, hearing the deafening ticking clock of their time together. Grasping for any way he could repair this before she was gone for another month.

"Hey, hon, what do you want to do next time? Maybe bowling? Or, what if we stayed in a hotel with a pool somewhere? You could invite a friend?" Even as he said it, he knew he couldn't afford it, but maybe he would find a way by then. He scurried to keep up with her. His knee was killing him, and he gritted his teeth with every step.

"Dad, actually I've been getting really behind on homework when I come stay with you. And all my friends live by Mom's house."

Those sentences terrified Ron, and he didn't want to ask more about what she was trying to say.

"Where's the car?" Gwen froze in place. Ron stood next to her, staring at the empty parking spot.

"Wait. I don't..."

"Did you park in front?"

"No, I parked back here." Ron looked around frantically, weaving through the tightly packed cars of the other residents. "I am *sure* I parked right here last night, Gwen. This can't be happening. I better call the police." Ron spun around to see Gwen pulling a taped sheet of paper off the back door of his apartment.

"What's this, Dad?" She handed him the paper.

Ron took the form and stared at it for a long time. Gwen didn't ask any more questions.

"Go inside and call your mom. She'll come pick you up."

Gwen didn't move. Ron looked up at her. "Go ahead. You can still make it to the birthday party on time."

He noticed something in her countenance had shifted from anger to pity. He wished she would go back to being angry. That was easier to fix.

THE GETAWAY CAR

The driver smelled like smoke and vinegar. He reached over to open the glove box and rifled through some papers. He found a deodorant stick and let it drop to the floor. He found half of a Hershey bar, closed the glove box with his pinkie finger, and began to eat the chocolate. Holding the bar in his mouth, he adjusted the radio with his free hand. From her vantage point, turned on her side in the back seat, Chare could see the man's ears were coated with yellowish-brown wax and thick dark hairs. After a few miles, he slowed the car and parked next to a phone booth.

"Yeah, I got the Ford Escort, boss. The dipshit left the keys in the ignition, so I'm driving it over to the shop now. Mark should be back with the tow truck in about an hour. He's gonna try to nab that Pontiac over on 7th Street."

Chare learned the driver's name was Steve, and he had been talking to J Green, the owner of a shop on Willis Drive. Greenie's Auto Salvage and Repair.

Every repossessed car and truck in the Bloomington area was held in a large parking lot adjacent to Greenie's for two weeks while the car's owner was notified and given one last chance to pay up. When the two weeks expired, J and his crew would get the car cleaned up and ready for auction. Small repairs, paint touch-ups, interior detailing, and sometimes new tires. Major repairs were rare. Chare noticed that some cars never made it to the auction house, and large amounts of cash were exchanged during whispered conversations.

For the next seven years, Chare sat in

the corner of Steve's cramped office in the back of the shop. A small black-and-white TV rested on her lap. A hand print of motor oil residue was still smeared on her neck from the day she had arrived. The office was often too cold, and the TV's electrical cord was a constant nuisance, but overall she was OK. Despite the occasional flashback to the infamous "Blood Game," and missing her family when she let herself think of them, she felt safe. She was glad she could be useful, holding the television.

Chare had learned about romance from *Days of Our Lives*. She knew the signs.

Steve had been flirting with Tammy, the bookkeeper, for months. Tammy seemed interested, too, but she had a boyfriend who worked next door at the scrap metal yard. The boyfriend had muscles bigger than Steve's, and a barbed wire tattoo around his bicep. Tammy, J, and a few others usually watched the soap opera in Steve's office while they all ate lunch. Tammy and Steve would sit next to each other on the edge of his metal desk, and sometimes share a sandwich. Chare noticed that Steve had been cleaning his ears and wearing polo shirts instead of grease-stained ringer T-shirts. He brought better and better sandwiches.

And this is how Chare finally moved again. It happened the same day Tammy announced she and the boyfriend were engaged. Steve had been out on a repo run when she told everyone at lunch.

"You hear Tam's engaged?" J said as he ducked his head in the door of Steve's office later that afternoon.

"Really? Wow. Good for them." Steve's voice sounded strange.

"Her rock is *insane*. There must be more money in scrap metal than we think."

"Right." Steve smirked. "Scrap metal."

"Say, can you close up tonight? I gotta drive to Chicago."

"No problem. I have paperwork to catch up on anyway."

Steve sat at his desk for hours. He didn't seem to be getting much work done. Chare watched him trace the business logo with his pencil over and over. Was this what heartbreak looked like? Everyone had gone home, and his green desk lamp was the only light.

But then, she was there. In the doorway. Steve looked up, startled. She wore a faded blue Pepsi T-shirt. He stood and walked to her. They kissed. They barely spoke as they undressed each other. Completely naked, Tammy and Steve walked to Chare's corner of the room. Tammy gently lifted the TV from Chare's lap and set it on the floor. She grasped Steve's shoulders, guiding him to sit down. And down he went. Chare was now more intimately acquainted with Steve than his doctor or his pajamas. What happened next was a dramatic and sweaty percussion of skin and saliva. A little motor oil on her back was now the least of Chare's concerns. But she watched with great interest. She thought she recognized Love, but maybe it was just a teammate of Love. The old injury in Chare's back left leg was aggravated again and again. And again. And again. It was particularly painful during the part when they stood up and both faced her. Tammy grasped the top of Chare and held it against the wall, which put enormous pressure on the point of the misaligned screw, digging it directly into the red plastic. But Chare found that after a while, she really didn't mind too much. This show was quite a distraction! Steve sat back down again and his body squished softly into Chare.

Tammy sat on top of him, this time turned to the side like a baby in his arms. Now Chare was sure she recognized Love. Despite the heavy weight on her, she felt no pain. They stayed like that for a long time.

Later that year, Tammy married her muscleman boyfriend. There was never another night like that one. Everyone from the office went to the wedding, including Steve. By all accounts, it was a very nice day.

Chare reflected on the moment Bobby had thrown her across the court. She had never had any empathy for him before. What he did felt so wrong. So brutal. But now, there was a small thought about the incident that was brand-new to Chare. Bobby had been so red hot and frustrated about the referee's call. Maybe sometimes the pressure becomes too great. Maybe sometimes there's nothing else that can provide relief. Nothing. Maybe once in a lifetime, just once, a person has to toss a chair.

After another three years of sitting in the corner and holding the TV, Chare fell in love, moved away from home, raised a family, and spent the rest of her life on the East Coast.

(What?)

(You'll see.)

"J, can you come down to my office? We've got a problem." Steve hung up the phone and started pacing behind his desk. Within thirty seconds, J walked into the office and closed the door behind him.

"What's going on?"

"You know that cherry red '65 Mustang convertible that's been sitting on the lot?"

"What cherry red '65 Mustang convertible? I have no idea what you're talking about."

"Funny. Well, I just got a very interesting

phone call. There's a movie production company filming in D.C. that wants it. And I mean *really* wants it."

"So, what's the problem? Sounds like a nice payday."

"They want it shipped out tomorrow."

"Shit."

"Yeah. We have two days left on the clock, so the loan payment could still come in. Not to mention if it does go to auction, it's basically promised to Vince."

"I'll handle it," said J.

"How? Vince doesn't get handled."

"Maybe I can convince him to come up to their price."

"Long shot, but even if he does, what about the two days? Do we stall these movie folks? They said they can have a truck here tomorrow morning, so the Mustang would be in D.C. for a scene they need to shoot Wednesday."

"What are we talking about here?" J asked.

"$30K."

"Damn." J leaned his head against the door jamb. "OK. I hate to do this, but let's Houdini this one."

"What do you have in mind?" Steve asked.

"Can you meet me here at midnight?" J grabbed a pen from Steve's desk. "Give the movie guys this address to send the truck in the morning. And tell them to use this bank routing number for the payment." J scribbled the information on a pad of paper. "Mustang 'gets stolen' tonight. New

VIN. Ships to D.C. in the morning. I'll file an insurance claim, the bank gets paid, everyone's happy."

"And what if the owner of the car ends up making his payment in time?"

"He won't. They never do." J turned to leave and then spun back to the desk. He reached into the pad of paper and ripped off the next 8-10 pages of blank paper beneath the top sheet, crumpled them and put them in his pocket. "Burn pile."

"Wait. Shit. I remembered something else," said Steve.

"What?"

"They require a chaperone."

"What the fuck are you talking about?"

Steve rubbed his temples. "They said someone has to ride along in the back of the truck with the Mustang."

"Fuck that. We don't need any more prints on this thing than we already have." J stood in place, thinking, rubbing his elbow with his opposite hand. He walked over to Chare and lifted the TV onto Steve's desk. "Put this chair in the back of the truck next to the Mustang in the morning. It will look like someone was back there the whole time. Add a Snickers wrapper for effect," J said, bemused at his own idea.

The plan went off without a hitch. J had been right that the owner didn't come through with a loan payment in time. The truck driver didn't ask questions, as he had turned a blind eye to much weirder and much worse over the years. Steve was able to strap Chare to the wall of the truck, facing the Mustang's driver-side door. He set an empty Fritos bag by her feet. The next day, Steve used part of his windfall to buy himself a wall-mounted color TV for his office.

It was love at first sight. Maybe it was his perfect shade of red. Maybe it was his panache. Any sentimentality or sadness about leaving Steve and the crew at Greenie's evaporated the second Chare sat down next to Mustang. The lines. The confidence. The sheer vitality. What she wouldn't give to touch that warm leather and that cool chrome. Chare didn't know how long it would take to get to D.C., or what would happen when they got there, but she knew they would enjoy the hell out of every single minute with each other on the way.

When the back of the truck was opened up, Chare knew she was not in Indiana anymore. The air felt different. The bushes were pink instead of green. Every day, hundreds of people rushed around, for hours on end, wheeling huge pieces of equipment and looking frantic. The red Mustang had been carefully rolled down a ramp from the back of the truck. Since then, Chare had only been able to catch a few glimpses of him. He seemed important to everyone there, especially Harry, one of the top dogs. Harry had been there when the truck was opened, all suntan and swagger, making sure the car didn't get a nick or smudge.

After a couple weeks, Chare had gotten used to hearing comments like, "Today we blow up the White House," and, "The aliens and the F-18s engaged in the largest air battle in history." The fellow who sometimes sat on her, and occasionally stood on her, was named Pete. Big ears, a baseball cap and a deep voice like a radio announcer. He was never far from his computer. Pete specialized in "compositing." He knew how to take a clip with a lot of people running for their lives, and stitch it together with a clip of *another* lot of people running for their lives, and make it look like the entire dang world was ending. Harry, despite being a movie star, took great interest in Pete's job and stopped by to chat almost daily.

"Say, Pete, I'm noticing it's an awfully hostile environment for cars around here."

"Yeah, you gotta wonder what the director has against them. Twenty-car pileup yesterday."

"Doesn't that get expensive?" Harry asked.

"Look around. Does it seem like they're pinching pennies?" As if on cue, three giant water tanks rolled by just outside the tech tent, with alien models submerged within. "Those will be destroyed by noon. And after lunch, they're bringing a troupe of Shakespeare players over from the STC to give you guys inspiration for the big speeches." Pete laughed. "Totally insane expenditures."

"What, you don't think they'll make the money back?"

"I have no idea, man. I hope so."

"Me, too. So, anyway, is it true another big car crash scene is coming up tomorrow? Do you have any intel on the '65 Mustang?"

"You're obsessed, dude." Pete pushed his chair back away from his computer and stood up. This was always the most painful motion for Chare. And she really didn't want to hear any more details about the terrible fate of her car. "Well, I know they've already got the father/son scene with that Mustang in the can.

I don't see why they can't crash it tomorrow."

"But wait, Pete. Wait just a minute, here." Harry raked his hands through his hair and paced around the small room. "I just don't get this. Can't you do the crash with digital models?"

"You want the art team to make photorealistic models of every car?" Pete laughed. "Harry, you're supposed to be the pro here. Do you have any idea how long these models take to create? I've been working on the digital net for this *one* crop duster for three weeks." He pointed to his computer display. “We haven’t even started on the exterior texture of it, which is all that really matters on screen.”

“What about physical models? Like the model they made of the White House?”

“Rare cases. Only when we can’t blow up the real thing. Making a hyperrealistic toy car is almost impossible. Just think about it.” Pete used his foot to move a computer cord away from Harry’s feet, then squatted down to tuck the whole tangle of wires more securely behind the desk. “Say, what’s your attachment to that Mustang, anyway?" Pete stood back up, turning to face Harry.

"Eh, it's just a thing in my head," Harry sighed. "I collaborated with a musician on my new album and that car just seems meant for her. I don't know how to explain it."

"Awww, Mr. Multi-Talented-Singer-Turned-Movie-Star wants to give his girlfriend a car? Yes, you're right, we should all stop what we're working on to make that happen for you. Jesus, you sound like a kid who's trying to swipe a souvenir from the set."

"It's not like that, Pete." Harry shrugged

and started to walk away. "I just wanted to thank her."

"Harry. Harry," Pete called after him. "Look, I'm sorry. I wish I could save the Mustang. But you gotta talk to the big guy. You know I don't make these decisions."

As Chare was learning quickly, sometimes in a crisis, it's not what you know, but who you know. Maybe more than just sometimes. The next day, Harry came bursting into the tech tent, whooping like a madman.

"Spared from execution by a last-minute

call from the governor!" Harry yelled, pulling the cork off a bottle of champagne under his arm. He grabbed two clean coffee mugs from the shelf by Pete's desk and filled them up, handing one to Pete. "The Mustang still rides. It's morning in America!" Harry was beaming, and Pete couldn't care less. The two men clinked mugs sloppily, and Chare felt the most incredible effervescent ticklish splash on the back of her neck. Relief. Gratitude. Bubbles. Joy.

And that night, for the first time, she saw fireworks.

“Can’t we take some junk, Mister? Come on, anything will do.”

“Sorry, boys, every single thing you see here is company property. Nothing leaves this set. Now get outta my way.” He pushed past them to a long table of discarded scripts.

“Even that?” one of the boys said, pointing to a hubcap lying on the ground next to Chare.

"Especially that," the man said, growing even more irritated.

"How is that possibly true?" the bravest kid asked again, not giving up.

"What's your name, kid?"

"John Piper, Sir."

"Look. John Piper. What if we have to reshoot a scene? We need everything to match perfectly. If we start letting extras take souvenirs, we'll never be able to find anything when we need it. Now, scram."

"But this is the last day of shooting. Everyone is packing up. Mister, we skipped school and took the bus all the way from Baltimore to do this today. Please."

"Didn't I tell you to scram?" The man walked briskly toward the boys, leaning forward with his clipboard jabbing the air. The boys took off running, heading in the direction of the bus stop.

"Wait! Wait!" The man called after them, laughing. "I have a souvenir you can take with you! Come back and get it!"

The boys stopped in their tracks and

turned around, excited, only to see the man had raised his middle finger at them.

Emerging from a hideout in the azaleas an hour later, one boy crept back to the set and grabbed a hubcap. Another boy swiped a call sheet. The third boy took a red plastic chair. Then: independent in movement but stitched together in purpose, the three boys ran for their lives.

THE PIPER FAMILY

Chare's time in the basement rec room would come to be defined by three memorable and nostalgic smells: Play-Doh, chlorine, and Saturday morning cinnamon rolls.

Mom was mad. At first, she seemed to have the calmest, most empathetic way of being mad. She looked at the boys kindly, and spoke in a normal voice. But the boys still looked terrified. John Piper, Cliff Piper, and a family friend, Michael, sat on the sofa braced for their punishment. Sandy Piper wasn't in trouble. She had been too young to tag along for the adventure, anyway. She opened three containers of Play-Doh and started to roll snakes on Chare's lap while sitting on the floor, cross-legged, listening in.

"You missed two swim practices. An entire day of school. If something had happened to you, how could anyone have come to help you? Nobody knew where you were. And where did you get the money for the bus to D.C.? Did you have anything to eat the whole day? Whose idea was all this?" Mom's eyes rested on each of them individually, her arms crossed.

Sandy Piper sat up on her knees in front of Chare, just a few feet from the sofa, twisted her colorful snakes into one megasnake, and worried for the boys. Already, a few tiny pieces of Play-Doh had fallen into the carpet by Chare's feet. The bright colors stood out against the dark maroon carpet, which looked like it could have been a remnant from a Chinese restaurant.

"Mrs. Piper," Michael began, before she cut him off.

"And now you pound a hole in my wall? And hang up a hubcap? Explain yourselves. What got into you? Have you lost your minds? Michael, does your mother know about all of this?"

"I…well, she's not…I mean…she's a big movie fan, Mrs. Piper."

"A MOVIE FAN? Well, slap my Rosebud and call me The Godfather. When you go to confession, will you hope your Priest is a cinephile, too, Michael?"

He stared at her, confused, and tucked his hands under his thighs. He looked quickly from side to side, hoping for support from his comrades.

"Mom, it wasn't Michael's idea." John Piper sat forward on the sofa. "It was my idea. I pretty much dragged them both along."

"How did you even hear about this?" She turned her full attention to John.

John looked to Cliff for help, and he jumped in. "We, uh, we saw an ad in the newspaper. They needed extras for a big scene. Mom, the world was ending! It was so cool!"

"Cliff, as 'cool' as that sounds, it was incredibly unsafe. As the oldest, you should know better, honey. I have to be able to trust you. *All* of you boys."

The three young criminals looked at their laps. The most wonderful smell began to waft down the stairs. Mrs. Piper left the room.

"Just hang on," John whispered. "It's almost over."

"You guys are gonna get it now," Sandy said. They could hear Mom coming back down the stairs. Using two potholders, she carried a glass Pyrex dish full of cinnamon rolls and a stack of paper plates under her chin. She set all of it in front of the boys, on the wood crate, which was covered in bumper stickers.

"Never again," she said sternly. She unplugged the video game controllers and cradled the mass of cords and devices in her arms. "You can have these back in two weeks," she said, and went back upstairs.

A relieved and smiling cacophony of, "Thanks, Mom! Yum! I'm sorry Mrs. Piper! Sorry, Mom!" chased after her as she shook her head. They couldn't see she was smiling, too.

The boys turned on the TV and gobbled up the rolls, fingers sloppy with frosting, ravenous after their morning swim training and the tense scolding. Saturdays were the only day of the week with just one practice. Every other day, they were all required to be back at the pool in the late afternoon. Sandy grabbed a warm cinnamon roll and set it towards the back of Chare's seat while she finished her creation, which ultimately became a barnyard pen, filled in with Play-Doh pigs and Play-Doh sheep. She adorned it with Easter basket grass, a Luke Skywalker figurine, and one menacing plastic dinosaur. Her damp pool towel hung over the backside of Chare while all of this was going on. Hours later, when Sandy was done playing, she took great care to gently wipe the plastic seat with the towel, except for a small frosting glop in the back, which she licked. Chare began to wonder if she had found a best friend.

Chare had been living with the Piper family for a year when Kimber, the springer spaniel, arrived. The chewing did not feel good. It did not feel good *at all*. And Kimber stared a lot. It was disconcerting. Kimber would curl up on the sofa and keep one eye open, aimed at Chare, for what seemed like hours until the kids came home from school or swim practice. And there was slobber. So much slobber. But after a few weeks, they seemed to develop an understanding. The chewing subsided (mostly) and Kimber was actually pretty funny sometimes.

"She looks like E.T.!" John said, pointing at Kimber. Michael had come over after training and they had built a fort using blankets and all the furniture, including Chare. The dog was under the fort with the kids and had gotten tangled in a blanket so that it hung over her head like a nun's habit.

"Coming through!" Mom called to them, carrying a laundry basket down the stairs.

"Mom, get in!" Cliff said, shouting through layers of fabric and cushions.

"No thank you, dear," she laughed, as she gingerly stepped around the tent city they had created.

"It's cool in here, Mom!" Sandy called to her.

"Coming through again, kiddos," Mom said, this time heading back in the other direction with a basket of clean laundry.

"Hey, Mom, can we have three or four towels? We have some gaps. I can see light," John said.

"No way, these are clean. Heading upstairs now. Remember: practice is at 2:00 p.m. today instead of 4:00."

The basement was quiet for a minute while the kids arranged the final details under the fort. But then they erupted in wild-man whoops and screams as they saw Mom slide under the fort, just between Kimber and Chare, a bath towel draped over her own head.

The years went by faster at the Piper house. Cliff had been away at college already for three years, studying engineering. John was about to leave, too. He would be starting film school in New York City. The basement rec room was lined with his packed plastic totes and piles of clothes. Sandy was now sixteen and didn't play on Chare anymore, but she would still rest her feet there while watching TV. That felt very nice. Most nights, Sandy came downstairs by herself to the rec room to watch David Letterman. Chare enjoyed Letterman, too, because sometimes he mentioned Indiana, although she felt sorry for all the watermelons who were smashed in the name of comedy. On weekends, Sandy's boyfriend, Brent, would come over and watch TV with her. Nobody else seemed to like Brent, including Kimber. Whenever Brent sat on Chare, he would lean way back on her rear legs, which was painful on Chare's old injury, and seemed risky for them both. Mom didn't like Brent because he didn't support Sandy's swimming. He tried to convince Sandy to skip practices, and he made fun of the sport. He didn't understand why she had to eat so many calories in her training regimen, and warned her she was going to get fat. The basement, for a lot of reasons, felt lonelier and lonelier.

But then one day, Sandy, Mom, and John came downstairs to the rec room, turned on the TV, and didn't leave for four days. At different moments, Chare saw each of them cry. Kimber was an older, calm dog now, and licked their tears when they let her. Chare had been facing away from the television when it happened, so she didn't understand, but she knew it was something very grave and painful. Everyone kept repeating one particular date on the calendar: September 11th. The more Chare heard, the more grateful she was that she hadn't seen what happened.

"Kids, let's take a walk or something. We have to stop watching this. Wanna go to McDonald's?" Mom asked.

"Brent's coming over," said Sandy.

"Oh, great," John said.

"What do you have against him, anyway?"

“Kids, don’t fight. We’re all on edge,” Mom said.

“Umm, maybe it’s that Brent is a total dickhead?”

“John!” Mom scolded.

“Well, sorry, but you know it’s true. You could do WAY better, Sandy.”

“OK, OK, kids. Cool it. Look, we all just need to get back into our routines. Sandy, the pool reopens tomorrow, right? John, have you heard from your college yet?”

"Yeah, we're supposed to report for classes next Monday. Sounds like most of the city is still shut down, though."

"And swim?" Mom turned to Sandy, but she didn't answer. "Honey? What about the pool? Do you know when they're restarting?"

"They, uh...they actually never closed."

"What are you talking about?" John asked her. "You've been home all week."

"I don't know...I just...swimming seems so dumb right now. Like, how can I go there and swim laps while all this is happening?"

"Is this Brent's doing?" Mom asked.

"I'd bet $1000," John said. Just then, they heard the front door open and Brent came down the stairs to the rec room.

"Wow, smells like ass down here," Brent greeted them. "Oh, hi, Mrs. Piper, I didn't see you there."

"Hello, Brent." Mom began to gather dirty plates and a pizza box to carry upstairs.

"Hey, babe," he said as he sat down next to Sandy and draped his legs over her lap.

"Yeah, could you not?" John said.

"What, John, are you gonna hang out with us down here? Huh," Brent nodded. "Kinky, but OK. But do you mind changing the channel? Kind of a downer, man."

"I have to watch this, Brent. I'm moving there in a week, remember?"

"Right, right. Whatever." Brent stood up and walked across the room to sit on Chare, and reached for the bowl of cheese popcorn. He ate the popcorn, wiping cheese dust on Chare's haunches while they watched a report on the spike in hate crimes across the nation.

"Fuckers deserve what's coming," Brent muttered. John looked like he was going to deck him. Brent chomped the popcorn faster and grosser, rocking Chare back on two legs, the bowl perched in his lap. Then he set Chare down flat and reached for a pool towel, tying it around his head like a turban. He went back to the popcorn and his two-leg tipping of Chare.

"Towelhead. Get it?" Brent laughed loudly

and Sandy looked like she wanted to disappear.

"Take that off, Brent. Now."

"I can't understand your words, John." Brent began ululating and making a praying motion as he rocked Chare. Chare felt something in her equilibrium hovering…like some deep core inside of her was resting on a gyroscope…as if she could go one way or the other…and for the first time in her life: By Choice.

The choice was easy. Chare sent Brent tumbling backwards. Hard. The popcorn bowl landed on his face. Sandy and John said nothing and didn't help him. Chare was hurt, too, but it was worth it.

Having her legs in the air like that must have made Chare's old injury visible to Sandy. She gently carried Chare over to the basement workbench in the adjacent room, used a Phillips head to pull out the screw that had been jabbing into her plastic bottom all these years, and realigned it into the proper threaded hole. Sandy also got a warm soapy rag and wiped off all the cheese dust, among other things. Sandy looked behind her to make sure the boys weren't watching, and then leaned forward and gave Chare a tiny kiss. She set Chare back in the TV area, gathered up her swim bag and went to practice.

After Brent left that day, Chare never saw him again.

It felt particularly cruel for Sandy to move away and for Kimber to die in the same month. Yes, of course, it was all good news, really, because Kimber had been hurting, and Sandy got a full ride swimming scholarship to Pepperdine in California. But it didn't *feel* like good news.

To Chare or to Mom. Two new "pets" had taken up residence on Chare's underside, but they were only spiders. Nice enough, and plenty entertaining, but Chare didn't want to get emotionally attached. Nevertheless, she named them: Backstroke and Butterfly.

The first week after Sandy was gone, Mom got a phone call from Michael, the kids' friend and old teammate. He was on his way back to college himself, and wanted to stop by that afternoon and pick something up. Within twenty minutes of that phone call, Chare could smell cinnamon rolls baking upstairs.

"Yes, yes, it's still hanging on the wall right where it's always been," Mom said as they came down the stairs.

"Ha! There she is! Cliff said it might still be down here. You sure you don't mind if I take it with me to hang in the locker room?"

"Not at all. That seems like the perfect home for it."

"I remember when you found out we all had skipped school that day. We thought we were dead meat." Michael carefully lifted the hubcap off its hook on the wall. Chare found this shocking. She and the hubcap had moved into the Piper house together. She thought she felt a hot prickle rising up in her as she watched this happen, but maybe it was just her spiders.

"I still can't believe you kids went to D.C. to be in a MOVIE without telling anyone," she shook her head and smiled. "What a riot you guys were. You sure kept me on my toes."

Mom and Michael stood quietly for a minute, not sure what else could be said to make it any easier to say goodbye.

"I suppose you'd better get going. It's

a long drive. Now, just promise me one thing, Michael," she looked at him seriously. "When you get there, you take the world by storm, OK?"

"I'm planning on it, Mrs. Piper."

"Good. Here, I'm sending you with these cinnamon rolls, too, dear. Maybe your roommates will like some."

"Really? Aww, thanks. You're the greatest. Sorry we gave you so much trouble over the years."

"Trouble?" Mom gazed around the

basement. "Oh, Michael. Hearing you kids laughing down here? It was simply the joy of my lifetime."

The day came when there were two Sandy Pipers. Well, one was a Sandra, technically. Chare got to watch the wedding video on TV. Everybody loved Cliff's wife. Both engineers, they were married almost immediately after college graduation and moved to Burlington, Vermont. News of Sandra's pregnancy came quickly, and Mom was over the moon.

"When was the last time we were all together?" John asked.

"It's been way too long," said Cliff.

"I can't think of a better occasion for a reunion," said Sandy, with her feet on Chare. "Wouldn't miss it for the world."

Mom walked down the stairs carrying a platter of Greek food: stuffed grape leaves, triangle-shaped spanakopita, chicken kabobs with tzatziki, and warm pita bread.

"Dang, Mom. Looks amazing." Cliff leaned

forward to admire the platter as she set it on the crate.

"Cliff, you might want to go help Sandra. She's bringing down more food and the baby is getting fussy."

Cliff popped up off the couch and took the stairs two at a time. John followed behind him to help as well. Cliff and Sandra returned quickly carrying the baby, as well as a tray of meatballs, hummus, and roasted peppers.

"I'm sorry, guys, but I need to nurse the baby. Is this going to be weird?"

Sandy took her feet off of Chare and scurried to get a blanket for Sandra. "Not at all! Of course not," everyone assured her. Sandra and the baby sat down on Chare, with the blanket draped over one shoulder.

"It's on!" Cliff yelled upstairs to John, who came bounding down the stairs with plates and a roll of paper towels. John sat down on the edge of the couch and reached for the remote to turn up the volume.

"Here we go," Cliff said, rubbing his palms together. "Come on, buddy."

Chare felt the baby's tiny hand grasp her side, fingers curled tightly. It was one of the best sensations Chare had ever felt. A drop of breast milk slid down the baby's chin and eventually landed on Chare's seat. The baby sighed and started to fall asleep. Sandra snuggled the blanket around her more securely.

"Pull!" John yelled, and the baby jerked awake momentarily and easily relaxed back to sleep. Her warm little fist still held Chare.

The Piper family sat together in love. They sat together awash in old memories and alight with new beginnings. They sat together with bellies full of the delicious food Mom had made in honor of the Olympic games in Athens, Greece. The Piper family sat together as they watched the race, hearts bursting, as their old friend, Michael, won the gold.

The family hadn't been all together again since that day, not even for Christmas. Mom was spending a lot of time lately cleaning the rec room and carrying things upstairs. She cried a little as she scavenged through a toy box, putting pink stickers on some toys, and putting others into a black garbage bag. At one point, she sat on the floor for an hour putting stickers on the corners of dozens of record albums, maybe hundreds. When she was done, she played Glenn Miller's "In the Mood" as she folded up the ironing board and moved it to the wall of the basement close to the staircase. As she walked with the board, she grasped it like a dance partner, and swung it around before resting it against the wall.

Then Mom walked over and put a sticker on Chare. She lifted Chare by her plastic seat and spun her around the nearly-empty room. They twirled together to the music, and Mom rocked gracefully from her toes to her heels, to one side then the other, smiling broadly. Her hair swung easily at her shoulders. Mom leaned Chare way down to the ground in a dramatic dip, and quickly back up again to resume the energetic bouncing rhythm. She pulled Chare in tightly to her left side, and then with one hand holding just one little silver foot, she flung Chare way out to the right side, not letting go. Chare was thrilled and unafraid. She thought about the night at the basketball game so many years ago, and how the very same flinging motion, but done with love, could feel so very different.

Mom danced Chare all the way up the stairs and outside to the driveway. Chare saw items from the house she hadn't seen in years. It was quite a reunion. The next day, a woman handed Mom one dollar and carried Chare to the back of her small purple pickup truck. Mom was helping the next customer, but she looked up when she heard the tires burn rubber as the truck drove away. Mom smiled curiously as she saw Chare slide from the front to the back of the cargo bed, slamming into the tailgate. As if the chair wanted to stay?

"Me, too," thought Mom.

YARN AND JUSTICE

A decade is a very long time to spend in a garage.

(Let's not discuss it, OK?)

One thing, though: Chare does not like spiders anymore.

The morning after the loudest of the screaming fights, the fight when the glass broke and the red and blue lights flashed from a car parked on the street, was the same morning Chare was lifted out from under a pile of forgotten objects in the garage, set down in the driveway, and sprayed with a hose. The initial blast was ice cold and pushed Chare over on her side. After all the cobwebs were washed away, Murph sprayed Chare all over with something that smelled like chlorine. Then Murph scrubbed around and inside all of Chare's nooks, turned on the hose again, and rinsed her off. The sun came out, and what had been a startling change now felt delightful. The warmth and the lingering scent, like swimming pool water, felt like a hug from her old friends.

"There we go," said Murph, as she wiped Chare down with a shammy. "Ain't you spick-and-span?" She lifted Chare into the cargo bed of a black pickup truck, which was much larger than the purple truck Chare had arrived in ten years before. Other things had changed, too. Murph's hair was shorter and turning gray. The house's paint was peeling, and the bushes looked overgrown. They drove for about an hour from Baltimore into the D.C. metro area, and parked at a large brick apartment building. Murph carried Chare up six flights of an outdoor staircase, stood on a small rectangular landing, and knocked on the metal storm door.

"Murphy! Child, what are you doing? Come in, come in!" A much older woman named Barb, white-haired and wearing a pink velour tracksuit, opened the door and ushered her inside. The apartment smelled like fried food was cooking, either right then or years ago.

"Mom" was the only word Murph could muster before tears overtook her.

"Oh, my girl! My sweet girl. It's going to be OK, doll. Now, just come in and sit down. Shh, Murphy, you're with Mama now." Murph sat down on the floral sofa and put her head in her hands. Chare remained in the doorway.

"Mom, I didn't know where to go," she sobbed. Barb poured Murph a cup of tea and sat on the sofa next to her, rubbing a hand on her back.

"You know you can always come here. I don't care how much time has passed. You know my door is open, child." Barb sat up straighter and set her own tea on the coffee table. "But six months, Murphy... not even a phone call...nothing. I've been worried sick...." Barb trailed off. Chare heard the pain in Barb's voice. Chare remembered the feeling of longing to have Sandy's feet resting on her seat, and the months of emptiness after Sandy went to college. It was a pain that felt worse than her old leg injury ever had.

"Well, you'll be happy to know she's gone. For damn good this time," Murphy said.

"Brittney? She's gone? Wow."

"Wow, indeed. And in dramatic fashion."

"Can you tell me about it, honey?" Barb asked.

Murph leaned back on the sofa with an exhausted sigh. "It was awful, Mom. I feel so ashamed. The cops came last night."

"Did she…hurt you?"

Murph hung her head. A full minute went by in silence. "She tried."

"Oh, Murphy." Barb put her arm around her daughter's shoulders and pulled her in close.

Murph pulled out of the embrace, leaned

forward, and tugged the side of her sweatshirt up to expose a large bruise on her ribcage, now yellowed.

"Lord Jesus, child! She did this to you?"

"A couple weeks ago. But last night…last night, she missed me," Murph laughed darkly.

They sat together quietly for a long time. Murph could finally hear the faint music from the kitchen radio, which must have been playing the whole time.

"I should go," Murphy said.

"No! You just got here! You can't go home. What if she comes back? Stay here, please. Stay as long as you need." Barb clung to Murph's arm.

"Mom, she won't come back. She cleared out. Don't worry. I can't be afraid of my home, and I have to work in the morning. I just wanted to see you."

"Promise you will call me if you need me."

"Yes, Mom. I will. But I'll be OK."

"Murphy..." Barb paused, looking at Chare.

"Can I ask...why do you have that red plastic chair?" They both laughed.

"Oh, sorry, I forgot about that." She was still laughing as she walked over and picked up Chare. "A pretty weird olive branch, huh?" She set it down next to her mom. "I know it wasn't very cool of me to be out of touch for so long. I'm sorry about that, truly."

"Honey, that's OK. But I was just so worried. Six months? I didn't understand what I had done."

"Look, Mom, you didn't *do* anything,

exactly. It's just...the last time we talked, I kinda felt like you had that attitude again...like that attitude you had when I first came out. I was getting the feeling that you didn't approve of my 'lifestyle,'" Murph rolled her eyes. "Or that I needed to explain myself. And I'm too old to feel that way anymore."

"Oh, Murphy. That's not the case at all. Please believe me, child. If I gave you that impression, it was only my reservations about Brittney, herself." Barb shook her head.

"I guess you were right about her, after all."

"I didn't want to be right, honey. I'm just sad for you. No olive branch needed," Barb put her hand on the back of Chare.

"Oh, right, the damn chair," Murph laughed again. "I remembered you said you used these types of chairs as frames for your yarn seat-cover projects. I don't know if you still make those anymore, but here ya go."

"Oh! Yes, it's the perfect size. And, you're wondering if I still make those?" Barb stood up and carried Chare to the bedroom. "Come look."

They walked into Barb's bedroom and

Chare could see about a dozen other chairs, all about her size, lined up along one wall. Each one was covered with an elaborate, colorful knitted work of art. Like chairs wearing sweaters. The knitwork covered the entire backs and seats, and then draped down, surrounding the legs, too. Some of the knit covers were woven geometric patterns, and some were designed to look like something realistic, like a bouquet of flowers.

"Damn, you've really been cranking these out!" Murph walked from chair to chair, examining the handiwork. "Any sales?"

"A couple. I take them down to the craft fair on the weekends and advertise them as car seat covers. Last week I sold one for fifty bucks and another for twenty."

"Not bad! Say, Mom, I could probably throw some of these up on Etsy. Maybe get more like eighty bucks."

"I don't even know what that is, Murphy. But, sure, you could try...if you don't mind. I love making them, but I'm barely covering the cost of the yarn."

"Can I take these fruit ones?" asked Murph, pointing to three car seat covers, designed to look like a pear, a pineapple, and a bunch of grapes.

"Oh, sure, anything you want. Those aren't my favorites."

Murph took out her phone and snapped photos of each cover, angling the chairs for the right lighting by the window. Then she carefully rolled the knitted covers up and off of the chair frames, shook them out, and folded each one carefully.

"If I get a sale, I'll mail it out to the buyer, and then send you the money, or bring you a check the next time I'm here."

"Thanks a lot, Murphy." Barb was excited. "I hope you're not doing all this for nothing. This will be so embarrassing if none of them sell."

"Mom, they're actually really cute. I bet they'll catch someone's eye. Plus, everyone likes to make their car a little cozier. If I still had my purple truck, I'd buy this bunch of grapes. But I don't know if any of these are the right vibe for my truck now."

"I take requests!" Barb said, so relieved her daughter was seemingly back in her life.

"Ha, I'll think about it. OK, I'm gonna head

out. I'll post these listings online when I get home. Will you be around this week? Are you still working for Ruth?"

"Yes, I'm still Ruth's morning caretaker, and they have a new guy named Branner who comes to relieve me around 1:00."

"Branner?" Murph laughed.

"I know," Barb shook her head. "He looks like he's about fourteen. Last week he told me he was late because his chinchilla escaped."

"Oh, Branner. Soldier on, buddy. Say, how's Ruth been doing these days, anyway?"

"Hanging in there. It's getting harder every day. But if there's anyone who might live forever, it's her. The Lord is watching over her, I just know it."

"I hate that you still have to work so much, Mom. I wish I could help you with money. I would if I could. You know that, right?"

"Don't be silly. I'm still strong. I like my work. And compared to Ruth, I'm downright young."

"Well, just promise me you'll retire before Branner does."

Murphy and her mom walked to the front door and gave each other a long hug. They both knew they would never go six months without talking to each other ever again. But as Barb watched her daughter descend the stairs and drive away in her black truck, she couldn't help but think the trouble with Brittney wasn't over.

Barb had been working for Ruth and her family for years. She helped Ruth bathe and get ready each morning, took Ruth through some simple exercises, and did some light cleaning. They were also good friends and talked extensively about life and ideas, despite their wildly different backgrounds. Ruth, now 87, was still living independently. In fact, until recently, Ruth herself was still able to work a few hours each day. Ruth's storied career had always been of utmost importance to her, and her family credited Barb for helping to extend Ruth's vital years. Sadly, Ruth's health had taken a turn, and the end seemed near. The family had hired additional nursing care in the home, and were preparing to say good-bye. Branner quit with no warning, and Ruth's family had asked

Barb if she would consider moving into a spare bedroom for two weeks to help provide comfort and companionship to Ruth in the final days. With no hesitation, Barb agreed.

Two weeks turned into two months, and then four, and then ten. Ruth was a survivor. Still reading and writing for part of each day, doing her therapies, and never giving up. Barb left for a few hours each weekend to go back and check on her own apartment. She had rendezvoused with Murphy a few times to give her more car seat covers, as each new batch continued to sell out online. Sixty dollars seemed to be the sweet spot for pricing. Barb was still barely breaking even on yarn costs, but it was a chance to see Murphy, which was worth everything. She seemed to be doing OK, but Barb was still worried about her.

The guest bedroom in the large house was just down the hall from Ruth. Barb spent most of her days tending to care needs, but she had some hours to herself at night to read and work on her knitting projects. Along with one suitcase of clothes and personal items, she had brought Chare along to use as a frame. Late one night, with her hands tangled in yarn, she heard

Ruth's bell ring down the hall. In her pajamas, and not wanting to lose her place, she grasped the sides of Chare, the knitting needles and yarn in a mass on the seat, and walked the whole thing down to Ruth's room. She gently pushed Ruth's door open with her foot.

"Miss Ruth, I'm sorry I'm in my bedtime clothes already. Can I help you?"

"Now what do we have here, my lady? What is this beautiful creation?" Ruth tried to sit up in bed to look more closely. Barb brought the yarn-cloaked Chare over to the side of her bed.

"My word, dear." Ruth reached her hand out to gently stroke the handiwork. "How amazing this is. You made this?"

"Yes, Ma'am. I've always done some knitting to take my stress down."

"This is exquisite, Barbara. The flowers. So many exotic flowers. It reminds me of a trip I took to Bali long ago."

"Thank you. I like this one, too. It's almost finished. My daughter has been selling them online for me. The colorful ones sell the best."

“Dear, can you adjust the oxygen? It’s too much, now. It all feels so dry.” Ruth struggled to speak as she tugged on her nasal tubes. Barb carefully sat on the very edge of Chare and helped to make Ruth more comfortable. She turned down the flow slightly, propped another pillow behind Ruth, and spread some ointment on her lips. There wasn’t much she could do, but it seemed to help.

“What will you make next, my dear lady?” Ruth asked.

“What would you like me to make, Ruth?

I take requests. I'll try to make anything you can think of."

"Oh, no dear, you make what's in your heart. That will be more beautiful than anything I could imagine." Ruth took Barb's hand. "Barbara, my friend. You have been my light these past few months. Your humor and your gentle care. I never deserved you, my precious lady." Ruth closed her eyes and placed her other hand on top of Barb's hand. "A mitzvah," she whispered. "A mitzvah."

The next day, Ruth slipped into a coma. Hospice nurses were taking care of her now, so Barb spent most of her time taking walks, preparing food for everyone, and in her own room, working on her final project: The Virgin Mary. In part, this project choice had been made simply because of her yarn shortage. All she had left in any sufficient quantity were blue, white, and a golden yellow color. But once she started knitting, she knew it was the perfect choice. Murphy wasn't religious, but Barb was planning to give it to her anyway. To watch over and protect her. Working on the intricate details day and night gave Barb comfort, too, in Ruth's final days.

Barb had missed a call from Murphy and played the voicemail message:

"Mom, I won't be able to make it over to your apartment today to pick up the next batch of covers. I…I'll have to get them another time. I'm sorry."

Barb's heart sank as she could tell from the tone of Murphy's voice that something was very wrong. She immediately called her back.

"I'm fine, Mom. I promise, I'm fine. You have your plate full, anyway."

"Murphy, I know you better than anyone. Please tell me what's going on. I want to help you."

"You've spent your whole life helping people. I can't take more from you. I'm forty-six years old, for fuck's sake. Sorry for cursing."

"That's OK, dear. Jesus had his earmuffs on for that one."

"But really. It's not your problem. I'm a grown woman. I can figure this out."

"Do you know that nothing gives me

more peace than when I can listen to you and help you? That's why I'm here in this world, honey."

Murphy sniffled, holding back tears. "Oh, Mama. I've really gotten myself into a jam this time."

"What is it? Did Brittney come back? Are you OK?"

"She did, in a manner of speaking." Murphy paused and Barb waited, bracing herself for the worst. "When she left last year, she cleared out our joint checking account. I didn't even notice until about a week later when my rent check bounced."

"That rancid bitch," said Barb.

"Mama!"

"Oh, excuse me. It just came out. But she is!"

"She is, yes. So anyway, I took some extra shifts at work and my landlord was nice about the whole thing. I got my name off our joint accounts. I've been digging myself out."

"Oh, Murphy, child. Why didn't you tell me?"

"Mama, no offense, but I know you don't got money. And it's my problem to solve, anyway."

"Please keep the money from Etsy, you hear me? Keep it all. I'll keep making more."

"Mom, this is bigger than Etsy could fix. They took my truck." Murphy started crying.

"What?"

"Today. They repossessed my truck. I was ninety days overdue…that was the last thing I was trying to catch up on. I just needed a few more weeks and I would have had the money, Mama. I've been working like a dog."

"Oh, honey."

"I went outside to the driveway to come to your apartment and get the next batch, but my truck was gone. That's when I saw the notice on my door. They took the truck to some repo lot downtown and I have two weeks to catch up on my loan or they'll auction it off."

"How much? Let me pay it for you, Murphy. I know you're good for it."

"Too much, Mama."

"Tell me."

"After all the fees, I'm behind almost $3000."

There wasn't much left to say but prayers. Barb told her daughter she'd try to think of something, anything. But she knew it was hopeless. She had never had three thousand extra dollars in her life. Barb hung up the phone and turned to face Chare. She grasped the sides of the knitted Virgin Mary and hung her head.

"Please, Lord. Please watch over my baby girl."

One tear landed on Chare, and was tenderly absorbed by the soft yarn of the Madonna.

Six days later, Ruth died. A flurry of family and staff filled the house, everyone tasked with too much. The funeral service would be well-attended, to say the least. Preparations were extensive, but Barb's role at the house was complete, and she had started packing up to move back home. The agency had matched her with a new job with another family that would start soon.

"What. Is. THAT?" Barb turned to her open bedroom doorway and saw a tall man wearing a dress and high heels, pointing at Chare.

"Oh," Barb looked at Chare. "Well, it's hard to explain."

"Please. I NEED to know." He came into Barb's room, uninvited, but she didn't mind. She had lost track of how many new people she had met in recent days. It was a revolving door of condolences and clean-up.

“It’s a chair. But, it’s the Virgin Mary. And it’s actually meant to be a cover you can put over a seat in your car. For comfort, I guess? Or just because you like how it looks?” Barb tried to explain.

“I need it.”

“I have others. This is the only Virgin Mary, and it’s for my daughter. But I have more for sale online. Fruit. Florals. You name it. Once I made a Hamburglar.”

"I'm dead. She said she made a Hamburglar."

Barb wondered who he was talking to.

"They're sixty dollars," she said. "I could reserve one for you if you want."

"I *need* The Virgin."

Barb turned back to Chare. "But, like I said, I made this for my daughter."

"I'll give you a thousand dollars," he said, with a dismissive wave of his hand.

Barb looked at him, stunned.

"You can't possibly mean that."

"My only job today is to inventory and appraise Ruth's art collection. I know what I'm talking about. And folk art is hot, hot, HOT right now. And this is just so... *cultural*. It's really incredible, you don't even know." He leaned in close to Chare. "Look at these details. It's like... perfectly hideous. And I mean that in the best way. Hideous can be *so* chic."

That didn't feel good. To Barb or to Chare.

"I can't even handle this," he continued. "Dearest brilliant Ruth, a world-class Jew, had a nurse down the hall knitting a big-ass Virgin Mary. It's too much. It is TOO much. Name your price."

Barb looked at Chare. She thought about Murphy. She looked at this man standing in her borrowed bedroom, being a complete asshole.

"It comes with a baby Jesus pillow for her lap," she said.

The man clasped his hands to the sides of his face in agony and ecstasy.

"Lord, forgive me." Barb closed her eyes. "My price is five thousand dollars."

"Sold."

Scotty wasn't really wearing a dress, he was wearing a kilt, his signature garment. At six foot three, he felt his legs were owed to the world. He placed Chare, in her Virgin Mary knitwear, just behind the driver's seat in his Sprinter van so he could see her in his rearview mirror. The rest of the van was loaded up with paintings, sculptures, and other valuable works of art. He slid the van door closed and spun 360° on the toes of his stacked-heel booties. It had been a successful day. His clients would be thrilled with what he was able to acquire from Ruth's collection.

"You won't believe what I picked up today," he said into the phone as he started the car. "I feel like getting sushi. Do you feel like sushi?"

Merging onto the freeway, Scotty adjusted his playlist and turned up the volume, feeling confident and alive. His art industry career had taken a circuitous journey, but he finally felt respected and ready for the next level. Scotty's sheer hard work and competency had, little by little, finally been enough to quiet the bigotry that surrounded him. He changed lanes to pass the row of cars in front of him. He couldn't wait to get home to see his twelve-year-old daughter, and celebrate with a sushi dinner. He tried not to leave her home alone for too long after school, but the project at Ruth's had taken longer than he had anticipated. He accelerated some more. An instant after he had cleared past the slower cars, a semi-truck heading the opposite direction lost control, crossed over the center median, and took aim directly at Scotty. Both vehicles were going over sixty miles an hour, and Scotty had no place to swerve. In the millionth of a second he had to react, he could see the truck driver's body slumped over the steering wheel, an image he would never forget for the rest of his life. Scotty turned hard to the left and screamed, crossing over the center median himself. Despite being rush hour, the lanes on that side were somehow empty, at least for the fifty feet he skidded and careened across them, spinning in a complete circle and coming to rest on the gravel shoulder of the highway. Chare was never worried; she had performed that trick before.

Almost five minutes passed before Scotty could move. He was frozen in place, one hand over his eyes and the other clutching the shoulder strap of his seat belt. When he finally regained lucidity, he felt something soft pressing into his right arm. He opened his eyes and saw the Virgin Mary had slid forward and was partly crammed between the two front seats of the van.

"GAWD!" Scotty yelled out in a rapturous bellow. He opened his door and walked around to the passenger side. Leaning across the seat to reach her, he gently rolled the yarn creation up and off of

Chare. He then placed it on the headrest of the passenger seat and slowly rolled it all the way down, tugging it carefully into place. He adjusted the Virgin's face so she was symmetrical and looking straight ahead. Then Scotty reached into the center of the van again, grabbed Chare by the neck, and removed her from the van. He discarded her on the shoulder of the road and drove away. The newly naked Chare was left for dead.

"Mary! Mary with the V-card! Macra-Mary! What do I call you? Forever my shotgun! Ride or die! You are NEVER leaving my side when I am driving, girlfriend. You saved my beautiful life." Scotty turned the music back on and started singing along as he pulled away and merged back into traffic, his heart still pounding.

"NOOOO," Scotty raked his chin with his fingernails. "Oh, Mary, what am I doing?" He quickly pulled back over to the shoulder of the road, and slammed it into reverse, shimmying his way back to the spot where he had left Chare. He got out, gingerly ran around the car to retrieve Chare, and tossed her into the back of the van.

"What was I thinking? This whole saga needs to be on TikTok."

Chare's rescue was short-lived, as Scotty put her out next to his garbage bin on the curb after he had finished creating the content about the "miracle," in which he mentioned Barb's Etsy account and directed his followers to "Make that gorgeous woman rich!" The Postmates food delivery guy arrived by bicycle, bringing Scotty and his daughter a celebratory feast of sushi and dumplings.

A minute later, out on the curb, there was another celebration of sorts. "Ha!

Oh, man, I have to show this to Ron," the delivery guy said to himself as he took out his phone and snapped a photo of Chare. "Hoosier pride, baby." He climbed back onto his bike but then stopped. "Wait a minute, maybe I can do one better."

He looked back at Scotty's house and then down at Chare, assessing her shape and weight. He quickly grabbed her by her metal back legs and propped her onto and over his handlebars, using strong fingers to hold her in place, and started pedaling. Slowly and carefully at first, the guy rode with Chare for about a block, and then adjusted her position so he could ride faster, eventually secure enough to make it up to his full speed. Chare couldn't believe the feeling of the wind as she coasted through the streets of Arlington, Virginia, speeding for miles into Washington D.C. After months of being covered in yarn, this felt like a jailbreak. They passed a large reflecting pond and an enormous monument that looked like a pencil. Then she saw the big white house she had watched being blown up, in replica, on the movie set years before. A lifetime of memories and joy rolled over her, and it was not diminished by hardships. It was not tarnished by moments of bad luck or even mistreatment. For the next few miles, she had a wind-whipping, eagle-soaring, front row seat to what it means to be truly alive.

"Oh, shit," the guy said, just as Chare started to feel the most deliriously spectacular sensation.

Rain.

RON

"Ronny, you're fired."

"You don't mean that," Ron said.

"Well, no, I don't mean that, but I've tried to tell you ten different ways that it's time for you to go, nicely, and you don't seem to be getting it. This is the last straw. You know I love you. We all do. But my hands are tied."

"Please, Marcus. I love my job. One more chance."

"You've used up all your chances, Ron. And buddy, you're seventy-five years old! You have thirty years in. Full pension. You'll probably make more money staying home than coming here."

"That's not the point, Marcus. I shouldn't have to retire before I'm ready. Was what I said really *that* bad?"

"Let's see here," Marcus said as he picked up the incident report. "Patron overheard employee A talking with employee B. A asked B why he was limping. B said he fell. A asked B how he fell. B said, and I quote, 'My erection was so big, I tipped over.'" Marcus set the paper back on his desk and looked up at Ron.

"People have no sense of humor anymore."

"Well, I agree with you on that," Marcus nodded. "But the Smithsonian Museum staff is held to the highest standards. There are kids everywhere. Dignitaries. This kind of stuff just doesn't fly. You've been here forever, Ron. You know all this."

"Things have changed, though. I used to be able to say whatever I wanted."

"Yes, Ronny. Things have changed."

Ron's co-workers took him out for burgers that night. Their boss, Marcus, had informed Ron he would have two weeks left. It was bad news for everyone, as Ron was beloved. Even the youngest staffers, only twenty-five years old, talked to Ron regularly, getting advice and simply enjoying his wisdom and humor. He was a heroic grandfather figure, and would be dearly missed around the museum.

Indiana University was playing a game on the big TVs in the restaurant. Everyone knew Ron was from Indiana, and had heard his story of the "Chair Game" multiple times. The topic came up again, and Theo, one of the young ones, had never heard about it. Another young guy, Casey, took out his phone and found the clip on YouTube. He set the phone in the middle of the table so everyone could watch Bobby throw the chair.

"Ha, look, the Purdue player runs over

there like he's gonna get the chair and bring it back to Bobby," Casey laughed.

"The ref says, 'Whoa, son, you stay here at the free-throw line.'" Ron said. "It was total mayhem. No one knew what to do next. Three technicals!"

"I wonder what happened to that chair," Linda said. "I bet they auctioned it off for some alumni fundraiser."

Casey took out his phone again to Google this. "Looks like no one knows what happened to it. Some people have claimed they had it over the years.

Supposedly there are sixteen of the chairs still there at Assembly Hall, from the original set of one hundred."

Ron was quiet and looked pensive. He ate his French fries and looked at the TV.

"You sure I can't get you a beer, Ron?" asked Theo.

"A beer? No, sir. I haven't touched the sauce in thirty-five years. Keep an eye on that pursuit, kids. What you're holding in your hand there is hell-bent on destroying your life. It won't always succeed, but it will keep trying."

"Geez, Ron!" Theo laughed. "It's just a beer."

"Would old Ronny lie to you? I mean, look, I wouldn't say it *ruined* my life, but it sure as hell changed it." Ron reached into his back pocket and took out his beat-up leather wallet.

Linda reached out her hand to shoo his wallet away. "Ron, you're not paying for anything tonight, hon."

"You bet your ass I'm not paying for anything tonight," he winked at Linda. "I just wanted to show you folks a picture of my daughter." Ron pulled out a newspaper clipping with a photo of Gwen on stage at the Kennedy Center.

His friends passed the clipping around the table, nodding and telling Ron how beautiful she was, and how impressive the article was. They weren't totally sure if they should believe him, and they exchanged some glances with each other. It could be a tall tale of a lonely man. But they went along with it. He passed around another small photo that looked like an elementary-school picture, maybe third or fourth grade. It had a thumbtack hole at the top.

"But she doesn't know me," he said, tucking the article and photo back in his wallet. "She lost touch with her old pops. I've written so many letters over the years. I'm not good at computers. She left when she was young...got a full scholarship to Interlochen. Her Mom wouldn't give me any info. You know how it is. But I couldn't be more proud of that girl." Ron started to choke up and Linda put her hand on his back to comfort him.

"Have you seen her play?" asked Theo.

"Dozens of times. I go whenever she's

playing in D.C. Even if I can't afford it, I find a way. I always wear a suit and tie, and take myself out for a piece of chocolate cake after the concert."

"That sounds really nice, Ron," said Linda. "I bet, in some way, she knows you're there."

Ron looked around the table. "Life goes by fast, kids. Don't wait to make amends. One month becomes one year becomes a lifetime." It was quiet for a minute. Ron assumed everyone sitting at that table was missing someone, or someone out there was missing them.

"Say, Ron," said Linda. "I was thinking, this doesn't seem quite right what Marcus is doing. Have you thought about calling a lawyer? You might have an age discrimination case on your hands." The other friends at the table seemed to agree with her.

"Really? Huh. I haven't considered it. Not sure where I'd get the money for a lawyer, anyway."

"I think those firms take these cases and you only pay them if you win," Linda said.

"Eh. What's the point? Marcus is right,

I'm seventy-five. What am I waiting for? I have to say good-bye sometime. At least he's letting me have the next two weeks. I never should have had this job in the first place, anyway."

"What do you mean?" asked Theo.

"Well, back in Indiana, let's just say, I had a bit of a record. Nothing crazy, but there's no way I could have gotten a government job like this. So, I might have fudged my application just a tad. And maybe even my middle initial," Ron laughed, remembering.

"I'm jealous of the old days," said Casey.

"Now the software can FIND YOU. It will always find you."

"That's true. It was a lot easier to disappear in the 80s. When I got this guard job at the Smithsonian, it was my second chance in life. A whole new beginning. The way things are now, it's harder for you kids to have the gift of a fresh start. You shouldn't be judged by one bad moment. Or who you used to be. Is anyone perfect? Come on. We all lose our persimmons once in a while."

The next day at work, Ron went back in to talk to Marcus, emboldened by the conversation the night before. He stopped short of threatening a lawsuit, but he was able to negotiate one very special parting gift. It took some convincing, but Marcus agreed. For the last two weeks of Ron's long career at the Smithsonian, he would be assigned to guard the one room he had never achieved the ranking to be able to guard. It contained the most popular and most adored exhibit: Dorothy's Ruby Slippers.

"Ol' Ron's in the catbird seat," said Theo, ducking his head in to see Ron at his new post. "You enjoying it, buddy?"

"Every minute of it. The only problem is, these two weeks are flying by. I'm done on Friday."

"Try not to think about that right now. But be sure to stop by the break room Friday. Linda said she's baking up a storm for your last day."

"Yes, sir. Wouldn't miss it." Ron moved slightly and looked like he was about to fall over.

"Whoa! Ron, hang on to my arm. Are you OK?"

"Oh, well, I feel silly now. Yes, I'm OK. Every time I see one of these kids click their heels together," he pointed to a group of children looking at the ruby slippers, "I try to do it, too. But it's a little tricky for an old man. I guess I'm not used to being on my feet so long every day."

"Take it easy, Ronny. No one needs you to go home just yet."

But he didn't stop. For the rest of his time there, when he saw a child click their heels together, he did it, too. Again. And again. And again. He had never had more fun.

One of Theo's many side-hustles to supplement his part-time job at the Smithsonian museum gift shop was delivering food for Postmates. He tried to take shifts at least three nights a week. The money was particularly good on nights the forecast was bad, and even though he delivered by bike, these lucrative shifts were always worth it. He had waterproof pannier bags that could hold even large food orders. Out on an order run the night before Ron's last day, Theo saw a red plastic chair discarded on the curb in front of a customer's house. It looked very similar to the chair everyone had been talking about at the restaurant. The one in the YouTube video from the Indiana game. It would make a hilarious going-away present. At first, Theo just took a photo of it to show Ron. But then on a lark, he decided he might be able to carry it home on his bike, and then take it on the Metro to work with him at the museum. The bike ride took forever, he felt ridiculous, and he got completely soaked to the bone in a rainstorm, but he did it. He rode the chair on his handlebars all the way home.

The next day on that train, Chare knew

she was headed somewhere new, but she didn't know where. She felt what could only be described as "change fatigue." What next? Who next? Would there ever really be a terminal station? A permanent family? A final assignment? Chare just wanted to go home.

"The kid's bringing his own seat!" a man called out to Theo as he stepped onto the train, and some others turned to laugh. He didn't know if he should set the chair on the floor, keep it up in his arms, or set it on top of another seat. He awkwardly held it in one hand while holding on to a bar with the other, and after a couple stops when there was more room, he set it down next to a row of seats.

"Trent, you in the mood, Cat?" The same man called across the length of the car to another man who was putting together a saxophone. He blew two times on the mouthpiece and played a quick flourish of a scale.

"I'm allllways in the mood, baby." Trent stood up and held court in the middle of the car as the next round of passengers stepped aboard. As the train pulled away, he started playing Glenn Miller's "In The Mood" to whoops and assents.

Chare knew this song. She thought about the time she danced with Mom Piper. Mom had seemed to accept that change was inevitable, even when you're not in the mood. The man danced with his saxophone in a similar way to Mom. He wasn't young, and it didn't matter one bit. He made his way down the length of the train car while playing the song, eventually setting one foot up on Chare for balance. He tapped his foot on her, along with the tune. Chare felt a drop of spittle land on her seat. Once again, unexpectedly and despite her fatigue, she found herself having a grand old time. Before reaching the Smithsonian stop and disembarking,

Chare heard an entire train car full of people, strangers to each other, manage to find a way to sing along to the last few bars of a wordless song. A song that couldn't speak.

(Pah pah pah pah Paaaaah!)

A black garbage bag covered Chare as she listened to the proclamation that was sent over from the Mayor of Washington D.C., read aloud to Ron at the morning meeting by Marcus, as they stood at the front of the break room. Ron choked up while listening to the words and "whereases," praising his years of service. Then Ron thanked everyone, especially Linda for baking all the treats. Chare thought she smelled cinnamon rolls.

"One more thing!" called Theo from the back of the room, dragging Chare up to the front with him. "You're not gonna believe this, Ronny."

"What's this?" Ron looked down at the garbage bag when Theo set it down next to him. "Am I about to smuggle out the Hope diamond? I knew I wouldn't get a gold watch, but this is too much!"

Theo returned to the group to watch the reveal, a big smile on his face. "I found this curbside, Ron, so don't get too excited," he laughed. "But I think you'll get a kick out of it."

Ron used two fingers to tug at the top of the bag, slowly revealing Chare. Everyone in the room knew the story, and their reaction was an utterance of "Ha!" almost in unison.

Ron didn't know, but Chare knew. Ron looked at the red plastic chair and laughed like crazy. He asked Theo more about how he had found such a close replica, and felt touched by the effort of hauling it on a bike in the rain and on the Metro that morning. It gave him a warm feeling that the guys around the museum really liked him, and hadn't just been humoring him. Eventually, Marcus wrapped up the event and told Ron to enjoy his last day, dismissing everyone to their posts.

But Chare knew. She knew right away. Ron looked almost nothing like he had at age forty, but of course she could never forget him. Chare didn't understand much of what had happened that night at the game, but she knew that Ron had somehow risked everything to save her from the man who had stashed her in the boiler room. He was her hero. Ron now tucked her under a table, grabbed a cookie and left the break room. But Chare knew their story wasn't over. She could feel her loop closing, like a bracelet about to be clasped. The table she was underneath felt like a protective bower, giving her a moment's rest in the shade before the final leg of her journey. She could feel her destiny and her home, pulling and yearning for her, just around the bend of time. And most of all, she could feel her little silver foot, hooked around the leg of another chair, start to warm up.

"Psst. Ron." Theo stood in the entrance to the ruby slipper room, right next to the corner Ron was standing in.

"Haha, what are you doing, buddy? You can't bring that in here," Ron said, cracking up again at the chair Theo was holding.

"Have a seat, my man." Theo set Chare behind Ron in the corner.

"You know I can't sit down, Theo. Marcus

would have an absolute fit. Guards have to stand at all times. Especially here." Ron gestured to the slippers.

"What's he gonna do? Fire you? Come on. You've been on your feet for two weeks. Cop a squat, Coach. This is your Hoosier throne!"

"Hoosier throne, huh?" Ron put his hand on Chare, and looked to his right and left, checking for consequences.

"It's even red, man. Fits right in. It's like it was made for this room."

"Well, you do have a point there," Ron

nodded, still reluctant. Theo went back to the gift shop and Ron stood in front of Chare for another hour or so. His shift was almost over. He had been checking his watch all day, wishing he could make time stand still. His feet hurt and his bad hip was giving him grief, even more than usual. With only a few minutes left on the clock, a little girl and boy entered the room, stood by the ruby slippers and clicked their heels together. Ron did it, too, two times. He almost lost his balance again. He decided, finally, to take a seat.

Ron gasped. The children at the exhibit turned around with concern. He smiled and waved them off, reassuring them. Ron closed his eyes. It was a gentle, perfect fit. A lock-and-key of contentment. Care. Warmth. Chare felt it, too. It was like she was made for him. The longer he sat there, the larger the notion of familiarity loomed. The notion of his life bending back upon itself. But it *couldn't* be the same chair. It couldn't even be from the same set of chairs. Ron stood up with difficulty, turned the chair upside down, and inhaled sharply when he saw the remains of the faint yellow markings of the words "Assembly Hall" printed across the seat's underside. He quickly put Chare back down and sat on her again, feeling flustered. But after a few more minutes sitting with her, so very comfortable, his unease turned to awe.

"It can't possibly be the same chair," he thought, as he closed his eyes again and smiled, letting his tired head slowly droop and rest on his chest.

(Sure it can.)

"Dad?"

Ron opened his eyes and looked up to see his beautiful adult daughter, Gwen, wearing a long teal-blue wool coat, holding the hands of a little boy on her right and a little girl on her left. The heel clickers.

He couldn't speak.

"Is that our grandpa?" the little girl asked, looking up at her mother.

Ron worked himself to a standing position, shocked, the beginning of tears welling.

"Gwen?"

"Yes, Dad. It's me. This is my daughter Joanie and my son…Ronald."

Ron carefully bent at the waist and shook both of their hands. "It's very nice to meet you." He stood and faced Gwen. "But how?"

"It's a long story, Dad. I saw you in the audience at the Kennedy Center. Well, I thought it was you, anyway. I called in a favor with the ticket office guys and got your home address. I went there, but turns out it wasn't your current address. The people thought you used to live there years ago."

"I want to show Grandpa my room, Mommy," Joanie said. "We can play with my toys." She tugged on her mother's coat.

"Not now, honey," Gwen said, squeezing her hand. "But, I kept searching. On and off over the months. And this week a mention of your name popped up on Google from a Mayor's proclamation for your years of service at The Smithsonian. The middle initial was wrong but I took a chance." Gwen looked at each of her children and then back to Ron. "So, here we are."

"I popped up on…Google?"

"Yes, Dad," Gwen laughed. "You popped up on Google."

"Will wonders never cease." The first set of lights dimmed in the room. All the other patrons were gone. In another few minutes, the rest of the lights would go out, too, except the security system.

"My shift is over, Gwennie. It's actually my very last day. I have to go. But please, can we spend some time together?"

"Yes, Mommy! Can we?" Little Ronald looked up at her hopefully.

"Well," she hesitated. "I snagged a good street spot. We could drive you home if you'd like?"

"That would be grand. Let me just get my coat in the break room." Ron hustled like he'd never hustled before. No foot pain. No hip pain. He was walking on air. He was so afraid when he came back out, they would be gone, but they were still standing there, right by the ruby slippers. He sheepishly walked over to

Chare and put a hand on her. He lifted her a few inches in the air and then set her back down. He looked at Gwen's face. She didn't seem to register anything about the chair. Was it possible she didn't remember witnessing that shameful tussle so many years ago? Or maybe it was her gift to him, to pretend she forgot.

"Is that yours? Let me carry it for you," she said.

Ron walked a few steps behind her as she carried Chare, and he held the hands of Joanie and Ronald. They left the museum, gliding past a moment he was now too distracted to be sad about, and walked four blocks to the car. Ron had no trouble keeping up with their pace.

“It’s a little cold, but should we put the top down anyway?” Gwen asked.

“Yes, Mommy!” the children squealed. Ron watched as Gwen lifted Chare into the middle of the back seat of a cherry red 1965 Ford Mustang convertible. Ron got into the front seat, and the children sat on either side of Chare in the back. They each held a silver leg. Chare detected notes of Play-Doh.

“What a beauty this car is,” marveled Ron.

His hand stroked the leather interior and the chrome along the dash.

"Isn't it great? I got this years ago. It was a gift from a singer after I collaborated on his album. It won a Grammy."

"Was it Harry?"

"Ha! Yeah. How'd you know?"

"I loved that album," said Ron.

"You really followed my career, didn't you, Dad?"

"Anything I could find, yes. Of course I did, Gwennie. I'm so proud of you."

"Thanks. Hey, you're not too cold, are you?"

"I feel warm, honey. I couldn't be better."

"So, Dad, what do you think you'll do in retirement?" she asked him.

"I'm not sure. I might start by taking a road trip back to Indiana." He turned his head to look in the back seat. "I have a little unfinished business."

After about fifteen minutes, they approached the parking lot of Ron's apartment building. Ron asked Gwen and the kids if they could come inside, but Gwen said maybe another time. She parked, and lifted Chare out of the back seat.

"Do you mind staying for just one more minute while I run in and get something?"

"Sure, Dad. We can do that."

Chare sat on the sidewalk waiting for Ron to return, admiring the love of her life, the Mustang. She sensed the feeling was mutual.

Ron felt light as a feather as he entered his building and ran up the three flights of stairs instead of using the elevator, taking the last flight two steps at a time. He was back down by the car in a flash and handed each child a butterscotch candy. They were delighted. Then he turned to Gwen, who was standing by the open car door.

"I have something for you, too, sweet Gwennie. Hold out your hand."

"Oh, Dad," she said, rolling her eyes and smiling. But she did as she was told.

Like a priest giving a Host to the faithful, he carefully placed the lucky guitar pick in Gwen's open palm. The guitar pick she had found at a Mellencamp concert in 1985. She stared at it for a long time, mouth agape.

"I know you don't need a good luck charm anymore. Obviously, you've made your own luck...."

"The guitar pick," she cut him off. "How did you...? But...how?"

Ron smiled at her. He had been imagining versions of this moment for thirty-five years. But this was better than them all.

"It can't possibly be the same one?" Gwen looked down at it in wonder.

"Sure it can," Ron said.

Sure it can.

THE END

While the location of the real red chair remains a mystery, many have claimed to possess it or know its whereabouts. Over the years, identical chairs have come up for sale, and Coach Knight signed one for a charity auction. At last count, sixteen chairs from the original set remain in storage at Assembly Hall in Bloomington, Indiana. Today, the Hoosier team bench is made up of a row of red, padded folding chairs. Their legs are tied together.

Also by Penn Anderson:

Brush: A Novel

"Life affirming. Page-turner." —*Kirkus Reviews*

"*Brush* is a stunning retelling of an ancient folktale. Get ready for the ride of a lifetime . . . *Brush* is a must-read for anyone seeking a heartwarming and inspiring story that will leave you captivated until the very last page." —*Midwest Book Review*

"Originality: 10 out of 10." —*BookLife Prize*

Available in paperback wherever books are sold

ISBN 979-8-9887493-0-1 (Large-print paperback)
ISBN 979-8-988-7493-1-8 (eBook)

www.ingramcontent.com/pod-product-compliance
Lightning Source LLC
Chambersburg PA
CBHW012032140726
47990CB00009B/3194

9798988749325